THE WITCH WHO SAVED CHRISTMAS

FELIX AND PENZI'S FIFTH PARANORMAL MYSTERY

KATIE PENRYN

Cover based on a design by
BOOKCOVERARTISTRY.COM

Published by
KARIBU PUBLISHERS SAS

THE WITCH WHO SAVED CHRISTMAS

Mpenzi Munro and her shapeshifting bodyguard Felix are once again called upon in the fight of good against evil. This time it is Christmas Eve. A vile and evil monster is trying to sabotage Santa's delivery of Christmas presents to the children of the world.

Penzi wants to stay home and have a family dinner, but Felix reminds her that a witch has to do what a witch has to do. Of course, Penzi does what she has to do with the help of the High Council of the Guild of White Witches.

~

ALSO BY KATIE PENRYN

Available from your favorite bookseller. Links on my website - KatiePenryn.com

French Country Murders

1 - The Witch who Couldn't Spell
2 - The Witch who Loved Éclairs
3 - The Witch who Got the Blues
4 - The Witch who Found a Pearl
5 - The Witch who Saved Christmas
6 - The Witch who Foiled the Plot
7 - The Witch who Hated Halloween
8 - The Witch who Risked the Shot
9 - The Witch who Picked a Poppy
In development:
10 - The Witch who Forged a Monet
11 - The Witch who Tipped the Scales

This series is available in Large Print and Ebook.

Our Man in Mazita

The WITCH who
SAVED CHRISTMAS

French Country Murders
Book 5

Copyright © 2016 by Katie Penryn

KatiePenryn.com

All rights reserved in all media. No part of this book may be used or
reproduced in any format, by any means, electronic or otherwise, without
prior written consent from the copyright owner and publisher of this book,
except in the case of brief quotations embodied in critical articles and
reviews.
This is a work of fiction. All characters, names, locales and incidents are the
product of the author's imagination, and any resemblance to actual persons,
places or events is coincidental or fictionalized.

Front Cover based on a design by
BookCoverArtistry.com

Published by
Karibu Publishers SAS

 Created with Vellum

CONTENTS

You will find Chapter 1 of the next book in the French Country Murders series, **The Witch who Foiled the Plot,** on Page 59.

There is a **Glossary** of French words and expressions used in this series on Page 71.

$\sim$

1

———

A sudden strong whiff of fish wafted past my nose, cutting through the incense of the Midnight Mass. All around me the congregation of the Roman Catholic church of Beaucoup-sur-Mer knelt in devotion as Father Pedro conducted the Mass on Christmas Eve. I raised my head and glanced around me to trace the source of what was becoming more pungent by the second. Far over on the other side of the aisle a group of fishermen from the port at Darennes offered the only explanation, but surely they were too far away?

MY FAMILY and I had moved to the Atlantic seaside town of Beaucoup-sur-Mer five months earlier after the news of my father's death. I'm Mpenzi Munro; my friends call me Penzi. My father, Sir Archibald Munro, had been a world famous anthropologist. He'd disappeared while researching the cannibal Wazini tribe in the Middle Congo. Rumor had it that he'd got too close to the subject of his research and

I

they'd eaten him. His will had stipulated that we should sell up our house in Notting Hill Gate, London, and move to France, to his holiday home which sat on the tip of the left-hand side of a perfect crescent bay, much loved by both French and British tourists.

Our mother had gone walkabout with a band of druids seven years earlier, leaving me to bring up my then eleven-year-old brother, Sam, and my two-year-old brother, Jimbo. So, when my father's will left no alternative I packed up the family and moved us with our two German shepherds, Zig and Zag, to *Les Dragons* in Beaucoup-sur-Mer. I had to give up my newly established practice as a barrister, but with years of schooling still to go for Jimbo, we needed a roof over our heads and the revenue from the trust fund my father had set up.

When we eventually arrived in the town aboard a tow truck, we found our long lost mother, Gwinny, staying in our hotel. She told us our father had left instructions and funds for her to renovate *Les Dragons* and turn it into a suitable dwelling for his three children. Jimbo was thrilled to bits to rediscover his mother while Sam and I treated her sudden reappearance in our lives with polite skepticism. Gwinny was repentant and lonely. What else could I do but invite her to share our home with us, at least until our lives settled down?

FOR THE PAST few months we'd made friends with the local townspeople and done our best to follow the adage of *When in Rome*. That's why Sam, Jimbo, Felix and I were attending mass at the local church although our family is not Roman Catholic. Gwinny had opted to stay home and prepare for Christmas Day. Oh, I haven't explained who Felix is. Felix was one of the two big surprises my father threw at me when he died. Felix arrived out of the blue as a beautiful Savannah cat. My father had sent him by special animal delivery from the Middle Congo. A few days after his arrival I walked into the kitchen at *Les Dragons* to find a handsome but unknown young man with tawny shoulder length hair and peridot colored eyes sitting at the kitchen table. It was Felix in human form. When he'd had a chance to reassure me, he explained that he was a shape shifter. I'd never met one before and wasn't even sure I believed in them. He tried my belief even further when he shifted into leopard form. Sir Archibald had sent me a shape shifting man-cat-leopard to be my bodyguard against all things evil in the natural world.

On to the second surprise left me by my father — the natural as opposed to the supernatural world. Apparently, I was a witch, a white witch, the genes coming down to me from my mother in her mitochondrial DNA. Over time we learned that Gwinny had been a feckless witch, but even so she gave me important advice from time to time. She had put me in touch with the High Council of the Guild of White Witches who were now supervising my training in witchiness. The Council had kindly made an exception for me. I'm dyslexic and so learning my craft from my mother's old *Book of Spells* was impossible. They had granted Felix permission to act as my helper. We made a good team, Felix and I. He taught me the spells as and when we needed them to fight evil and restore good, and I cast them. To date that had involved solving several murders and bringing the perpetrators to justice.

Along the way we'd established a sometimes rocky relationship with the mayor, Monsieur Bonhomie. Tonight, he'd invited us to share his family's Christmas dinner after the Mass. Sam and the mayor's daughter, Emmanuelle, were good friends, so Sam was looking forward to spending the Christmas celebration with the Bonhomie family.

I WRINKLED my nose as the fishy pong grew in pungency. What could it be?

2

___

Sam hadn't noticed the odor, but Jimbo had.

"Penzi, what's that stink?" he asked me.

"Shush," I replied. "You mustn't talk in church."

Jimbo shuffled about on his seat and gave Felix a nudge. Felix gave me a sideways look and raised his eyebrows.

"Fish?" he whispered to me. "Here in church?"

I shushed him and tucked my head back down on my hands on the back of the pew in front of us.

As I did so, I caught a movement out of the corner of my eye. Instead of closing my eyes in prayer again, I opened them wide and looked about me under the row of chairs.

A scruffy and mottled tabby cat, his large head crisscrossed with scars, was slinking his way forwards under the chairs. At that moment the prayer ended and the congregation as one rose from their hassocks and sat back on their seats. A tentative claw raked down the back of my calf, catching for a moment in the denim of my jeans. I jerked my leg aside and flapped my hand under the chair to shoo the cat away. He changed tactics and squeezed himself out between my legs and Felix's. He turned round and sat back on his haunches looking up at me from his position beside my feet. Felix nudged me and I gave my shoulders a polite shrug. The cat rubbed himself against my knee and mewed softly.

"Shush," I said to him, patting his head.

That's when I recognized him. It was Neptune, the king of the cats down at the fishing port of Darennes. He ran the security patrol for the fish market and the warehouses, keeping the rats away. We hadn't seen each other for some time which is why I hadn't known who he was straight away. That and the incongruous context of this meeting — at Midnight Mass several miles away from the harbor.

Felix whispered, "It won't be much longer. See, everyone's going up for communion."

We waited quietly for the service to finish, Neptune watching me all the time through slit eyes as if he wanted to make sure I didn't escape before he had the chance to make his business known. The good citizens of Beaucoup-sur-Mer poured out of the church sweeping us along with them. The first snow of the winter had fallen during the service. As I stamped my feet and rubbed my hands together, Neptune hooked his claw in the hem of my jeans and gestured with his head round to the side of the church. Once we were out of sight, I picked him up and asked him why he wanted to talk to me. We had to make sure no one was watching or within hearing because only supernatural beings can talk to animals, and no one in Beaucoup-sur-Mer knew I was a white witch, apart from my mother Gwinny and my two brothers.

"I'm sorry to disturb you, Penzi, but you did say that if I ever needed you, I had only to ask," he began.

I nodded.

"Well, we need you now — urgently — down at the harbor."

"Can't it wait? It's Christmas Eve. The mayor is expecting us for *Le Réveillon* at his house. We shouldn't offend him by not turning up or by being late."

Le Réveillon is what the French call their Christmas dinner. It usually takes place late on Christmas Eve to early Christmas morning. In our case after the Midnight Mass. Being invited to the mayor's house for such an important family feast was a great honor and it wouldn't do to disappoint him.

Neptune stroked his whiskers with his paw and shook his head.

"I wouldn't be here if it wasn't a matter of the direst import," he said. "You could say the happiness of the world depends upon your helping us tonight."

"Can you tell me what it's about so I can judge for myself whether tomorrow would do or not?" I asked him.

He pushed himself out of my arms and landed on the ground with a muffled meow of protest.

"Absolutely not. I'm honor bound not to speak of it outside our warehouse down at the harbor. It's a matter of such secrecy that if the news got out—"

Felix bent down to talk to Neptune at his level. "Will it take long?"

Neptune rolled his front haunches and began to lash his tail from side to side as cats do when put under pressure.

I crouched down beside Neptune and stroked him from head to tail until his fur lay flat again.

"I'm sorry, Penzi. It's impossible to know how long it will take you to fix this problem... or if you can. It might simply be without a solution and then heaven knows what's going to happen to us all."

Felix gave me hand to help me to my feet.

"What do you think, boss?" he asked me.

I looked down at Neptune. "Would you say it's a matter of good against evil?"

This time Neptune arched his back and hissed at some invisible peril behind him.

"Most definitely," he said. "Please come with me now."

"Felix?"

"We have to go. It's your duty as a white witch to fight evil whenever called upon to do so."

I sighed. "I know, but I was hoping for a quiet family Christmas with no disruption."

Felix chuckled. "A witch has to do what a witch has to do, boss."

"You don't have to remind me. The situation calls for the *obliviscere* or *forget* spell. I'll have to make everyone forget the passage of time while we attend to Neptune's emergency. When it's over we can hurry across to the Bonhomie's house and join in the dinner with no one being any the wiser."

"Can you remember the spell?"

I nodded.

"What about me?" Sam called out from behind us.

"And me?" Jimbo asked.

I'd forgotten about Sam and Jimbo. They were both gawping at us as if they couldn't believe their eyes or ears.

"Shall I ask the Bonhomies for a lift and take Jimbo with me?" Sam asked.

Felix looked down at Neptune. "Do we need an extra man?"

Neptune pussyfooted through the snow to Sam and looked him up and down.

"He's part of your family, Penzi? He knows you're a witch and that you can talk to animals?"

"Yes, he's my brother Sam."

Neptune's tail swished while he weighed up the danger of a security breach against the bonus of an additional strong human being.

"He comes with us," he said and walked back to Felix and me.

"And Jimbo? We can't leave him here on his own, Neptune," I said.

Neptune looked back over his shoulder at Jimbo who was doing his best to look tough.

Beckoning my brothers with a claw, the bossy cat said, "I suppose the little one could come in useful."

Sam and Jimbo hurried across to join us. It was forbidden for them to see me cast a spell so I asked them to close their eyes.

"Cross your fingers, too, both of you. Felix, you know what to do. And pick Neptune up and cross his paws. We don't want the spell to work on you four as well."

As soon as they were ready, I summoned up the mental energy to cast the spell, took a deep breath to flood my brain with oxygen. I uttered the magic words and envisioned the magic symbols.

With Felix carrying Neptune we rushed to the car park and jumped into our car. I drove as fast as I dared at that time of night on roads covered with fresh snow.

3

———

When we reached the harbor at Darennes, I switched off the engine. Our car stood alone in the car park at the end of the quay, its engine steaming in the cold air. Anyone who didn't have to work on Christmas Eve was at home with their family. Neptune meowed to be let out of the car. He jumped down into the snow which came up to his elbows as he high stepped over to the wall of the warehouse.

"Come along," he called back. "Every second counts."

Jimbo and Sam followed him over to the darkened building.

Felix pulled me out of the car. As he shut my door behind me a sudden gust of wind blew my knitted cap off my head. I struggled to maintain my balance, and my cap flew over to the edge of the quay. I chased after it and lost my footing in the fresh snow. I skidded forwards and would have fallen into the icy cold waters of the Atlantic if Felix hadn't caught hold of me in the nick of time. As we stood teetering on the brink gulping in the wintry air, something brushed against my face gusting a foul stench.

Felix drew me away from the edge.

"Did you feel that?" he asked me.

"And the smell. What was it?"

Felix shook his head. "No idea. Something rotten floating in the harbor, perhaps."

Over against the warehouse twenty yards away, Neptune let out an earsplitting caterwaul and flinched, flattening himself against the wall. With Felix holding my arm to keep me on my feet, we struggled through the snow to join him.

"We must hurry," Neptune said.

He sidled along the wall towards the giant doors leading into the fish market, shrinking his usual macho posture down to the ground.

"Too slow," said Felix, letting go of my arm and picking Neptune up. "Phew," he said. "Now I'll stink of fish, too."

Neptune squirmed in Felix's arms. "This is no time for joking or insults, sir."

As we made our gingerly approach to the man way cut into the main gates, I imagined all the possible reasons for Neptune's anxiety and his appeal to us for assistance. Maybe one of the female cats in Neptune's gang was having difficulty delivering her litter of kittens. Maybe the gang had been badly beaten up by a rival gang. Maybe the rats were back in unmanageable numbers. Maybe someone had attacked and abused one of his team, and he wanted us to help find the culprit. Nothing I imagined prepared me for the strange scene that met my eyes as I stepped through the man way into the warehouse and snapped on my flashlight.

For a few seconds my mind stopped working, and I rocked backwards in shock. Sam and Jimbo gasped. Felix, who was a step behind me, grabbed hold of me to steady me.

I closed my eyes and took a deep breath. Perhaps I was hallucinating after all the incense in the church.

But no. When I opened them again, they were still there. A group of reindeer. Reindeer in the fish market? They stood in defensive formation with two of their number facing outwards to ward off attack, typical herd behavior when threatened. A sleigh with golden runners and scarlet panels, its seats piled high with packages and parcels of all shapes and sizes came next. I blinked and looked further along. An old man sat on an upturned wooden fish crate his head cradled in his hands and bowed low over his knees. Was I dreaming? In his ermine trimmed red coat and hat, he had to be Santa Claus.

So deep was his dejection, he didn't raise his head until I tapped him gently on the shoulder. He swept his face up to look at me. Gone was his famous twinkle. Unshed tears glistened in his eyes.

Before I had a chance to speak Neptune ran forwards and rubbed himself against Santa's worn black leather boots.

"Your Lordship, this is the young witch I told you about, Mpenzi Munro. She's here to help you, sir."

Santa pushed his hood back and ran his hands through his sparse snowy white hair, shaking his head from side to side as he did so.

"No one can help," he moaned. "My magic isn't strong enough this time. I'm defeated."

Over to the left the reindeer jostled each other, their winter hardened hooves clicking on the concrete floor. Their sentries blew out a harrumphing grunt of warning. The smallest deer bleated and pushed her way into the middle of the group. Our entrance had disturbed them. Were we friend or foe?

Santa caught me watching his reindeer, and he gave a heavy sigh.

"That's my problem. It's never happened before. They're on strike. My reindeer have gone on strike. They refuse to take another step outside this warehouse. How am I going to deliver Christmas presents to the children?"

"Why have they gone on strike, sir?" I asked him.

He ran his hand down his long white beard as he gazed over towards his precious team.

"They're terrified about what's been happening to us, but they won't discuss it with me."

"Let me see what I can do," I said standing up from my crouch beside the old man.

Felix began to follow me, but I stopped him. "No, Felix, not this time. Reindeer are prey animals and you're a carnivorous hunter. You'll only scare them more."

Felix shook my hand off his arm. "Boss, I'm only a carnivore when I'm in my leopard mode and even then not a practicing one. I never eat when I'm a leopard. When have you ever seen me chase and hunt down a prey animal?"

I had to admit I hadn't. Felix the leopard had threatened and even on occasions attacked the murderers we had come across in our investigations, but he had never killed and eaten an animal or a human being to my knowledge.

"That's as may be, Felix, but this time please hold back. You'd be better off giving your support to Santa. How about some of your Laphroaig?" I asked him and patted his pocket where he kept his trusty silver hunting flask.

Felix went nowhere without his favorite tipple, the peaty single malt from the Isle of Islay.

He turned back to Santa and drew out his flask. I watched him pour a generous tot for Santa who accepted it gratefully and drank it down in a flash. Sam and Jimbo hadn't left the doorway, too awed to make a move. I waved at them to accompany me and carried on towards the reindeer who were now crowding into the corner of the warehouse fronted by their sentries, one of whom had a large shiny red nose.

Jimbo hurried to catch up with me, brushing snow off his copper hair as he ran. He tugged at my sleeve. "It's Rudolf. You know Santa's famous reindeer – from the song."

"Gently, Jimbo. You'll startle them all. Stand quietly."

I walked up to the deer with the red shiny nose. "You must be Rudolf," I said holding out my hand for him to sniff before I stroked him between his ears and down towards his shoulders. "I'm Mpenzi Munro. I'm a white witch, and I've come to see if I can help you all."

"We can see you're a witch," he snorted, "but this may be way beyond your powers."

"Why don't you introduce the rest of your team to me and then we can talk things over?"

One by one Rudolf called the others forward, eight in all. Donner, the second sentry, was the leader of the team.

"My mate, Blitzen," Donner said encouraging one of the shivering females to approach me.

After I'd stroked her nose, four males came up to me and said hello: Dasher, Prancer, Comet and Cupid. That left the last two girls. Vixen skipped up to me, but Dancer hung back. No amount of coaxing from Rudolf would make her leave her corner. She pushed herself back into the walls as if trying to disappear.

"Is it all right for me to approach her?" I asked Rudolf.

He nodded his head and the bells on his antlers tinkled. "You'll see why she's so scared when you get up close."

I gestured to Sam and Jimbo to stay where they were.

Rudolf and Donner kept up their vigil to the front, eyeing the two boys but deciding they posed no threat. The others turned to watch me as I began my oblique approach towards Dancer with my hand held out palm up. For my first couple of steps she followed my progress, but suddenly she took fright, tossing her head making her bells ring. I took a step closer. She snorted, showing me the whites of her eyes in warning. I halted and waited for her to calm down. When she'd settled, I moved slowly forwards and held out my hand to her.

"I'm Mpenzi Munro," I said. "A white witch called in to help sort out your team's problems, so you can fulfill your destiny and make the children of the world happy when they wake up tomorrow morning."

"My name's Dancer," she said. "I'm glad you're here, but there's nothing you can do. Look," she said turning her right flank towards me.

4

———

A claw had gouged deep into Dancer's flesh, all the way down from her spine to her knee joint. An attempt had been made to clean the wound. I guessed Santa was used to doctoring his animals, but what alarmed me was that the striations had to have been made by an animal with nine claws on one foot, a giant foot at that.

I glanced back at Rudolf who'd turned from his sentry duty to watch Dancer's reaction to me.

"You see," he said. "The Snarl did that."

"And this," Dasher called out, bobbing his head to show me something had torn away half of one of his antlers. "The Snarl did that when I tried to defend Dancer."

Cupid pushed through his colleagues and lifted up his hind hoof for me to see. Something had bitten a chunk of flesh away from his leg.

"The Snarl again?" I asked.

They all nodded their heads settings their bells a-jingling, the joyful Christmas carillon at odds with the evidence of the Snarl's attacks on their team.

"Who or what is the Snarl?" I asked.

At my repeated utterance of the name, they shrank back into their defensive positions muttering and bleating amongst themselves.

"Rudolf?" I asked again as he was the boldest of the team.

He shook his head and rolled his eyes.

"We don't know. We've never come across it before. We call it the Snarl because it prefaces its attacks with a great snarling and growling, but we can't see anything. It's all around us enveloping us in a miasma of unbelievable stench."

Prancer inched forwards to join Rudolf.

"Sometimes we catch a glimpse of black swirling wings as it swoops down on us, then it's off again tossing us about in the vortex of its passage, blowing us off course."

"And the attacks are increasing," added Rudolf. "We've lost our faith in Santa's ability to protect us while we work. Of course, we want to deliver the Christmas presents to the children, but not at the cost of our lives."

Donner rubbed up against Blitzen.

"We have a new calf this year, our first. He's back in Lapland with Mrs Claus. We don't want him to be an orphan. Carrying on with tonight's delivery while the Snarl dogs our every move is a risk we're not willing to take."

Dancer edged out of her corner and bleated for attention.

"You can have no idea how scary the Snarl is. It creeps up on us. The first hint of an attack is the smell, but we can't tell what direction it's coming from. A whirling blast tumbles us all about. I'm frightened that it's going to spin us away in a tornado."

I rubbed her nose and stroked her back, taking care not

to touch the seeping wound on her flank. She'd been brave to leave her corner to talk to me.

"Well, guys and girls," I said stepping back away from the team. "You stay here and keep safe while I talk to Santa. My friend Felix and I will do everything in our power to help you through this."

Santa's face brightened as I walked past the sleigh towards him with Sam and Jimbo following along behind me. The Laphroaig had worked its own particular magic and cheered the old gentleman up. Felix told Sam and Jimbo to fetch some empty fish crates to use as seats and to stay quietly by the sleigh without interrupting while I talked things over with Santa. Felix kicked a crate over to me. I sat down facing the old gentleman.

"Well, sir," I said, taking his gnarled hands in mine. "They've told me about the Snarl and its attacks."

"So that's what they're calling the monster?" He bobbed his head in agreement. "A good name. It comes out of nowhere making the most fearsome noise, blows us all about and lashes out at my reindeer whenever it can."

Felix crouched down on his heels.

"I guess it's a new phenomenon, sir?"

Santa nodded.

"It first appeared somewhere between Asia and Arabia. I didn't pay much attention at first. We often encounter strange gusts of wind on our travels." He broke off and glanced from Felix to me. "How much do you know about my job?" he asked.

Felix nodded at me. "Over to you, boss. This is more your field than mine."

"Every Christmas Eve you and your reindeer visit the homes of all the children who've been g—"

"Not all children," he said. "But we can talk about that later."

"Who've been good," I continued. "All year long your factories in Lapland make the toys you'll deliver on Christmas Eve."

"And my elves work in the factories," Santa said.

"And your reindeer are magic on this special night of the year, so magic they can fly through the skies." I let go of his hands. "But I've never understood how you can visit everywhere in a couple of hours."

For the first time since we'd come upon him, Santa smiled.

"Ah, Mpenzi Munro, you're forgetting about the rotation of our planet around the sun. We set off after midnight on Christmas Eve, flying down the International Date Line in the Pacific Ocean just east of New Zealand and Russia. We work our way through the homes of the children who live to the west of the line. We fly up and down the lines of longitude, gradually moving west as the planet turns to the east."

"So, you are always travelling at the same time of the night, in the hours between midnight and dawn?" Felix asked.

Santa smiled again. "Exactly. We have twenty-four hours to complete our trip."

He fell silent and his shoulders slumped again. "But not this year. My team is stuck here in the South West of France. We've covered only half the world, give or take a degree or two. If I can't persuade my reindeer to continue, I shall disappoint all the children living in the west of the United Kingdom, on the islands of the Atlantic Ocean, in the countries of South America, the United States, Canada, and those who live on islands in the Pacific Ocean east of the date line."

He groaned and dropped his head into his hands again.

I jumped to my feet.

"There's no time to lose. We have to tackle this dreaded Snarl and stop it from sabotaging your important work." I sank back down onto my crate again. "But how are we going to do that? I'm all out of ideas."

Felix put his arm around my shoulders.

"You'll think of something, boss. How about your *Book of Spells?* Perhaps there's something suitable in there."

"Oh Felix. If only— but it's back at home. We don't have time to drive all the way back there, fetch the book and then for you to teach me a new spell. And we don't even know if the spell would work."

"Next best solution: ask the High Council of the Guild of White Witches for help. If ever we needed their powers of good magic over evil, it's tonight."

5

"Why didn't I think of that?" I asked and checked my watch, catching sight of my brothers' faces as I did so.

"Remember," I said to them. "This is all top secret. Not a word to anyone when this is all over."

"I promise," said Jimbo.

"As if," said Sam giving me an eye roll.

I turned my attention back to the time. "It's too late to summon the High Council. We have to do it at midnight, and we were at Mass then."

"If the reindeer would agree, they could fly us west until we hit midnight again," suggested Felix.

Donner let out a loud grunt. "We heard that. There's no way we're moving from here until you get rid of the Snarl."

"So many if's, and time is passing," I said. "I vote we go for it and try to summon the Council even though it's past midnight. Have either of you got a better idea?"

Both Santa and Felix shook their heads. Rudolf called out that the reindeer were so scared they couldn't put two thoughts together.

"Right," I said, taking charge of the situation. "To summon the High Council of the Guild of White Witches we need: cognac—"

"We don't have any," said Felix.

"I drank all mine before you arrived," Santa said. "What we need is a St. Bernard to come strolling through the door."

Felix laughed. "The way the snow is falling, one may come along any minute. But there again," he added as he turned serious again, "we've only been using cognac because we're in France. Witches in other countries must use their local spirit. Tequila in Mexico and—"

"—Scotch in Scotland," I finished.

"Exactly," he said fishing his flask out of his pocket and shaking it. "There's just enough left for the summoning ceremony."

"Where are we going to find a sprig of bay leaves?" I asked.

Neptune stepped forwards. "I can help there. I'll send one of my minions round to the back of the warehouse, to the bay tree that grows there."

"Fine. Do it now and hurry him up."

"A silver goblet for the whisky," added Felix.

"Done," said Neptune. "There's a football trophy in the Harbor Master's Office. I'll send a couple of my team to fetch it. They can get in through the cat flap."

I clapped my hands, forgetting in my excitement that I'd frighten the reindeer who started bleating and making soft little grunts of alarm. Santa called out to them that there was nothing to be afraid of, and they settled down again.

Felix took out his mobile phone, saying, "I'll find the nearest dolmen. There's got to be one close by. The countryside is littered with them."

"Why do you need a dolmen?" asked Santa.

I shrugged. "Just one of those things. We have to perform the ceremony at a dolmen. My mother, Gwinny, who is also a witch though not a very effective one, says it's because they're ancient monuments dating back to pre-history, and they represent the portals between this world and others, such as the realm of magical possibility."

Felix swiped his phone off. "Found one. Only ten minutes away. It's do-able even against the ticking clock."

"Oh heavens," I slapped my hand to my forehead. "We've forgotten the most important ingredient, and we don't have time to go home and search for one."

"The diamond," said Felix.

"Yes, I forgot about that. Where are we going to find a diamond at this time of night? We're in a fish market, for heaven's sake," I said as my euphoria at finding a solution gave way to a feeling of hopelessness.

A deep voice spoke from behind me. Santa was back from calming down his team of reindeer. "Perhaps I can help there."

"Yes?" asked Felix, barely keeping the skepticism out of his voice. He glanced down at Santa's hand. "You're not wearing a ring I see."

"No," admitted Santa, "but I'm sure to have a piece of diamond jewelry in amongst all the gifts piled up in my sleigh. It's just a question of finding one."

Felix gave me a nudge. "Penzi can use her *veni metallice* spell. The spell works like a metal detector. Any piece of diamond jewelry will be set in a precious metal."

I found myself jumping up and down. "Felix, you're brilliant. That would never have occurred to me."

"You make a good team," said Santa leading me over to the sleigh.

"Everyone shut your eyes," Felix called out. "No one's allowed to watch Penzi cast her spell."

I hoped I'd remember it. I took a couple of deep breaths. My brain needed the oxygen to boost my magic energy. The symbols surfaced in my memory and the magic words rose to my tongue. I cast the spell and hurried over to the sleigh anxious to find a diamond as quickly as possible. I waved my arms slowly over the piled up gifts, but it soon became clear that such a mountain of possibilities was confusing the workings of the spell. My arms twirled so madly they were in danger of shooting out of their sockets.

Felix provided a practical and speedy solution. He organized Santa, Sam and Jimbo into unloading the sleigh and setting the packages out in a line along the floor of the market. I started divining for precious metal at the end nearest the sleigh. Several objects were turned up: gold watches, but they were all digital so no diamonds, gold earrings, bracelets, silver tableware and so it went on. Halfway down the line my hands took on a life of their own. We'd found a 24 carat necklace with a solitaire diamond pendant the size of a robin's egg.

"Quick," said Felix picking it up. "Anyone got a knife. We have to prize the gem out of its setting."

"Let me," said Sam taking the jewelry from Felix and unhooking his knife from his belt.

The cat who'd been sent to fetch the bay leaves had returned during our hunt for the diamond, but we still awaited the couple who'd been dispatched to fetch the silver cup.

Felix took the diamond from Sam. "Go down to the Harbor Master's Office. I suspect the cats are having trouble carrying the cup back here."

Sam raised his eyebrows. "Where is it?"

"Out the door and down to the last building. You can't miss it. The *tricolore* will be rolled up on the flagpole above the front door ready to be unfurled tomorrow morning."

Felix, Jimbo and I sat down on our fish crates again while we waited for Sam and the silver cup to arrive.

"Who exactly are you taking with you to summon the High Council, boss?" Felix asked.

"Santa should come with us. He'll be able to make his case better than us," I replied.

Santa gasped. "I can't leave the reindeer alone. They're frightened, and the Snarl might manage to find a way in here."

I looked at Felix. "It would be best if you stayed behind to guard the reindeer."

Felix shook his head with vigor. "More than my life's worth. I'm your bodyguard, boss. I stick with you come hell or high water."

"You're my protection against the dangers of the mortal world, not the supernatural world. You wouldn't be any good against the Snarl. It can't be a natural creature. The more I hear about it, the more I'm convinced it's a force for evil sent to destroy the joy children experience on Christmas morning."

"Amen to that," said Santa.

"Felix, surely nothing in the natural world is going to attack me between here and the dolmen, and back?"

"I'm not prepared to take the risk, and that's final," he said.

The three of us could take Jimbo with us and leave Sam to guard the fish market, but I doubted whether he'd be able to mount much of a defense against the Snarl. I tried once more to get Felix to stay behind reminding him that I was protected from supernatural evil by the *semper tuens* spell which cast an apricot colored aura around me as a cone of protection. The High Council of the White Witches had given me permission to learn the Level Four spell when the witch doctor of the Wazini had made attempts to attack me.

Felix wouldn't budge. "Boss, you know very well that spell hasn't been working properly recently. It's due for its weekly repetition. I'm coming with you and that's that."

After discussion we decided that Sam should stay and bar the doors while we were gone. Santa coaxed his reindeer into a circle behind the sleigh, their antlers pointing outwards. Neptune called his cats together and positioned them in a magic ring around the reindeer as reinforcement.

Scarcely had we arranged all this than Sam walked through the door with the two cats in his arms and the silver cup poking out of his coat pocket. We gave him his instructions, packed the ingredients for the summoning of the High Council of the Guild of White Witches into one of Santa's empty sacks and left the warehouse. Holding Jimbo's hand I slipped and slid my way through the now freezing snow to our car. Santa was too big to sit in the back, so he took the passenger seat while Felix and Jimbo sat behind me with the sack between them. We turned out of the car park onto the road and had gone an icy hundred yards when Felix cried out, "We've forgotten something."

"No we haven't," I said.

"Boss, we don't have a natural creature with us."

"Won't I do?" asked Santa.

Felix and I looked at each other for a moment before shaking our heads. "I'm not sure," I said. "Aren't you a supernatural?"

"Oh yes, I forgot about that."

"What about me?" asked Jimbo.

"No good," answered Felix. "You're a human being. It has to be a creature from the animal kingdom."

There was no help for it. We had to turn round and drive back the way we'd come. This time I risked driving along the icy quay right up to the doors of the fish market. Felix rushed inside and came out with one of Neptune's tribe tucked into his coat, saying that Neptune himself had to stay and look after his gang. I made a dicey K-turn on the frozen quay and tore off onto the road. A flash of movement caught my eye in the rear view mirror. The cat Neptune had deputized to accompany us poked his head out of the Felix's coat. Hardly a cat. He was the tiniest kitten, pure black save for a splash of white between his ears.

"Keep your eyes on the road, boss," Felix called out in alarm as the car threatened to skid into the ditch.

"But he's such a cute little thing," I said as I switched my attention back to the road in front of us.

A high pitched voice from behind me said, "My name is Martin, madame, and I'm strong. I want to help *Le Père Noël*."

Santa turned round to the back seat and tickled the little fellow under the chin. "Thank you. I'm glad to have you on my side. You're a brave cat. As for me, I'm apprehensive about meeting the High Council."

Felix held the kitten up to the window to watch the countryside whizz past. To Santa Felix said, "They are scary, I grant you, but as long as you mind your P's and Q's, you'll be all right."

6

Exactly ten minutes later we drew up outside a darkened service station where only the brand sign shone down on the pumps.

Santa peered out at the oil smeared forecourt. "It can't be here," he said. "How could a portal to other worlds be in such a dingy place?"

Felix checked his phone and the GPS on the dashboard. "It's here all right. Drive round the back, boss."

The car bounced over the uneven surface bobbing the headlights up and down until we turned the rear corner and the tarmac evened out. The now steady beams of light picked up the dolmen set diagonally across the far rear corner of the property, up tight against the security fence.

Santa leaned forwards in his seat to get a better view. "It doesn't look promising, Penzi. Quite insalubrious, in fact."

Santa had a point. The staff had been using the dolmen as their smoking area. Cigarette ends and snack bar wrappers lay inches deep at the foot of the dolmen's two upright stones. Someone had built a pyramid of beer cans on the topping stone.

I switched off the engine, leaving the headlights on to light the scene. "We don't have the time to be fussy, sir. And would you mind taking the sack of magic ingredients? Felix has Martin to look after."

Jimbo climbed out of the car after Santa, his eyes wide with excitement at staying up so late and finding himself in the middle of a magic adventure. I considered telling him to stay in the car, but couldn't bring myself to spoil his fun. I hoped the High Council would forgive me for introducing another natural human being to witness their appearance in our world. They'd been angry about Felix the first time the two of us had met them.

"Jimbo?" I called back to him. "Please stay close to Santa and don't speak whatever happens."

"Oh I won't," he said and held onto Santa's coat until we reached the dolmen.

Santa helped me place the bay leaves, the diamond and the silver cup on the top stone. Felix passed me Martin, took his flask out of his pocket and poured what was left of his precious Laphroaig into the cup.

"Ready everyone?" he asked.

Santa hoisted up his bulky red coat, planted his feet apart and hooked his thumbs into his belt. "What do we do now?"

"Penzi and I will light the whisky and then walk three times round the dolmen in a clockwise direction. You might want to close your eyes on our third lap, sir."

Santa screwed up his eyes, looked from Felix to the dolmen and back again. "How are you going to get round that thing? In case you haven't noticed whoever put up the fence has left you no room. You won't be able to get past the corners."

True. The problem had flashed across my mind as we

walked towards the dolmen, but in the muddle of preparation, it had disappeared. Now, I examined the fit of the dolmen against the property division.

Looking back at the others, I pointed to the way the top stone overhung the sides. "We're lucky. We can squeeze through under the overhang at the side. So, are we good to go?"

Everyone nodded. I passed Martin to Santa who stowed the little fellow away in the voluminous folds of his coat and wrapped his spare arm round Jimbo's shoulders. Felix warmed the sides of the silver cup with his lighter before tipping it over to light the surface of the whisky. The blue flame flickered and danced.

"Quick before it dies down," he said, grabbing my hand and pulling me along after him under and around the first corner, round the back and under the second overhang to the front again. Three times we performed the circuit. As we finished the third, a loud crack sounded through the cold night air and a flash of eye-dazzling brightness illuminated the scene. Santa jumped back and in the silence following the commotion I heard little Martin mew with fright. We all blinked to recover our sight and stared at the space in front of us.

But... it was still empty. There was no one there. Our summons had not been answered.

"Oh Felix. It's too late," I said. "They won't come. It's half past one in the morning. What are we going to do now?"

The anti-climax overwhelmed me. Seconds earlier I had anticipated a quick solution to Santa's problem. Now we had nothing left to try.

Santa put his arms around me and gave me a bear hug, almost squashing poor little Martin who meowed in protest.

"It's not your fault, Penzi. You did your best."

"But all those children are going to be so disappointed. And what's more," I said stamping my foot. "That nasty Snarl and its master have won. I hate that. I hate to see evil win over good." A sob of anger broke free. "And we wasted a diamond. Makes me furious."

Felix paused as he collected the silver cup to stow it away again.

"Boss, have you considered asking your mother for advice?"

"Yes," said Jimbo. "You could ask Mum. She's wiser than you think."

Oh, not again. My relationship with my mother had not been an easy one since she reappeared in our lives after an absence of seven years during which it was left to me to bring up my two younger brothers. I bore a grudge against her for robbing me of my youth even though I knew she was desperate for us to be friends again. Nowadays, we coasted along living in the same house but without any depth of affection.

"Penzi," said Felix again, pulling me out of Santa's reassuring embrace. "Phone Gwinny... now! You have to put your childish hurt aside if you want the children of the world to have the Christmas they're expecting tomorrow."

"How's she going to help?"

"She's been a witch for longer than you. She may know something you don't. After all, it was Gwinny who first put you in touch with the High Council."

I wasted another half a minute thinking over what Felix had suggested. "What if she minds being woken up at this time of night?"

Felix's reply was a snort of exasperation. "Boss, don't disappoint me."

Santa joined in saying, "It's the season of goodwill to all men. That includes wayward mothers, Penzi."

I had to try. I took out my phone, swiped it open and called my mother. Of course, I woke her up. It took me some time to explain the situation to her. It's not every night a mother gets woken up by a daughter who's trying to save Santa's reindeer from an invisible monster.

"I get the picture, Penzi," she said. "It's an emergency of the utmost urgency. You have to call the High Council's hotline."

"What? They have a hotline?"

"Of course. This is the twenty-first century. If you call ooo-ooo-HECATE, you'll get through to their emergency answering service. There's always someone on duty to ensure the fight goes on against the evil in the world." She paused. "And Penzi?"

"Yes," I said.

"You are looking after Jimbo, aren't you?"

"Of course, I am."

I nearly said I'd done it well enough for seven years, but I bit my tongue. As Santa had said, it was the season of good will.

7

———

The answering service put me straight through to the secretary of the High Council. It took me a few precious minutes to persuade her to report my call for help to the other members of the High Council.

"It's Christmas night," she said with a whine in her voice.

"You've hit the nail on the head," I replied. "It's now or never. We can't have a Christmas Day with no presents for the children."

"Very well," she said. "We'll be with you as soon as I can arrange it."

"Don't you want to know where I am?"

"No. I have your GPS co-ordinates."

And with that she closed off the call.

"Well?" asked Santa, Felix and Jimbo together.

Before I had time to answer, a great whoosh of colored light closed in on us, blinding us for the second time that night. When our eyes settled down, we saw before us floating above the dolmen the seven witches of the High

Council of the Guild of White Witches seated around their conference table.

"Who dares to call us out on this cold Christmas Eve?" asked the Head Witch in a disgruntled tone. "It had better be serious."

Jimbo flinched against Santa's side.

I took a step forward and looked up, making eye contact. "It's Mpenzi Munro, your Ladyship."

"What is it this time? Not more trouble with that meddlesome witch doctor?"

"No. This time the problem has worldwide implications, your Ladyship."

I waved Santa forwards to stand beside me. The Head Witch did a double take as she gazed down at him.

"Is that Santa Claus?"

Santa bowed his head just a tad, enough to show respect but no more. "It is, your Ladyship."

"From one supernatural to another, I bid you welcome, sir," she said. "But I'm puzzled as to why you're not circling the globe with your team of magic reindeer on this Christmas night."

"Perhaps I could explain," I began.

"Let the old gentleman speak for himself, Mpenzi."

Santa bridled at the epithet of *old*. I took hold of his hand quickly and tugged it to warn him to mind his P's and Q's.

The secretary took a sheaf of papers out of her briefcase and passed a page out to each of the other six witches.

"I've consulted the latest intelligence reports and summarized the problem here, your Ladyship," she said.

The Head Witch held up a finger. "Just a second Santa Claus, while we read these notes."

Santa turned to me and shrugged. I shrugged back. We

couldn't risk hurrying them if we wanted them to help in time.

The furrows on the Head Witch's forehead deepened as she read down the page. The other witches tutted and fussed with their cloaks. At last the Head Witch raised her head and looked down at us.

"This is truly an unprecedented problem, not only for tonight but for the power of good in the long term. We shall have to get to the bottom of who or what has let this monster — the Snarl you call it? — free on the world. And tonight of all nights. The perpetrator has to be the most evil spoilsport the world has ever known."

Santa nodded. "He wants to destroy the joy and happiness of children all over the world on Christmas morning."

Martin who'd stayed snuggled against Santa's chest chose that moment to pop his little head out of Santa's coat. The Head Witch spotted him and pointed down at him. He shrank back for a moment, but then stuck his head out again and mewed.

"That's your natural?" the Head Witch asked.

Santa tried to push Martin back into his coat and said, "Yes, your Ladyship. He's only a kitten and doesn't know how to behave on solemn occasions like this."

"Pass him up here," she said, giving the secretary a nudge.

That meant climbing up onto the dolmen and handing the kitten up to the secretary of the High Council. Poor old Santa was much too portly to manage such an athletic feat, so it fell to Felix to take Martin from him and climb up onto the dolmen's top stone. As the secretary accepted the little cat, the witches all began to ooh and coo.

"Cute little fella."

"What a darling."

"How I love black cats."

And other remarks of the same ilk drifted down to us.

Martin lapped up the attention. He sashayed up and down their table purring his little head off.

That's when Felix nearly upset the proceedings. He took a step towards the dolmen. "Ladies, please may I remind you how urgent this matter is? The clock is ticking away. Santa has only this one night to complete his task. We have to find a way to neutralize the Snarl so the reindeer will break their strike and return to work."

The Head Witch jerked her head up and scowled down at Felix. "I've warned you before, young man, about speaking before you are spoken to. Don't presume to tell me what to do. What you don't know is that all the time my colleagues and I have been petting little Martin here, we've been consulting telepathically on the best way forward."

Felix bowed low. "I beg your pardon, your Ladyship. Please take my temerity in speaking to you uninvited as a token of my deep commitment to helping Santa and his reindeer combat the evil of the Snarl."

The Head Witch allowed the hint of a smile to reach her eyes. "Apology accepted."

She looked round the table and each witch nodded in turn.

"We have made our decision," she said. "Listen carefully for time is short. Come closer so I don't have to shout and place your hands on the stone. Not the boy."

So she had noticed Jimbo who was doing his best to hide behind Santa.

"Don't be frightened, child," the High Witch said to Jimbo. "We don't bite. I'm sure your sister had a good reason for bringing you along with her. Stand there quietly while we get on with our magic business."

"Shall we approach now, your Ladyship?" I asked.

"The quicker the better. You're fighting the clock, aren't you?"

I nodded and the three of us edged forwards. As we came up against the dolmen a surge of energy like pins and needles pulsed from the stone through my fingers and up my arms. Santa and Felix let out a small gasp at the same time, so I guessed the same thing had happened to them.

The Head Witch laughed. "Did you feel the magic power?"

We all said, "Yes, your Ladyship."

"Good. Here's what's going to happen. You'll return Santa to his reindeer," and she smiled down at Santa. "We are not able to destroy the Snarl for you now. The fight against evil has to be fought if the fruits of the struggle are to be worth anything."

Santa sagged against me. I gave him a sideways push, and he straightened up.

"Wait for it," I whispered.

The Head Witch continued, "We have endowed Felix with magic powers to enable him to champion the safety of Santa and his team against this monster. Felix will have to fight, make no mistake about it, but it will now be an even fight. Felix is to shape shift into his leopard form and fly escort alongside the reindeer team. To keep him warm, when you pass over the colder countries, he will grow a snow leopard's coat. You, Penzi, will ride the lead reindeer — Rudolf?"

Santa nodded.

"Penzi, your aura will keep you warm. Your part in all

of this is to show the reindeers there is nothing to be afraid of. Do you understand all that?"

"Yes," we three said in unison.

The Head Witch held out her hand to the secretary who passed her a box.

The Head Witch took out a jar of ointment and passed it down to Santa. "This is a magic unguent to smooth on the reindeers' wounds."

Santa thanked her. She drew out a bundle of ribbons and handed them down to me.

"Mpenzi Munro. Here is a medallion for you to tie round each reindeer's neck. You must tell them it is magic and will ward off evil. That isn't true, of course. If it was there would be no need to fight evil; everyone would simply wear a charm. However, you will find the placebo effect will take place, and they will become less fearful."

She turned to Santa again.

"I leave it to you, sir, to make sure that they all get home safely when all this is over."

"I'll take care of it," said Santa with a beaming smile.

"Mpenzi Munro, I expect the full story of the night's events from you along with your apprentice's weekly email report."

I curtsied and turned to leave, remembering Martin at the last moment.

The Head Witch smiled. "Here you are," she said. "He'll make a witch a good cat some day. Take care of him. Now, good luck with your venture. I expect our intelligence reports to mention happy smiles all round tomorrow."

And with that the seven witches of the High Council vanished in a puff of smoke.

"Phew," said Santa. "They're scary ladies, but their

hearts are in the right place. Do you think we can do everything they said, especially you, Felix?"

Felix held his hand across his heart. "I will do my best."

"Forwards, everyone," I said. "We have everything we need to make Christmas work."

It wasn't until we reached the car that I realized the headlights were no longer shining.

I halted mid stride as my stomach somersaulted.

"Oh no," I cried as I opened my door and threw myself into the seat. I turned on the ignition. The engine didn't respond. As I feared, the battery was flat.

I raised my hands in despair.

"Hey guys, it's flat. What now?"

Poor old Santa who was half in and half out of the car, jumped all the way out again. "Nothing to it. Felix and I'll push you."

Felix handed Martin to Jimbo and joined Santa at the rear of the car. My car was a heavy old family station wagon. I glanced back as I put the car in gear. Santa's face grew redder with every yard. I hoped the car would start before he had a heart attack. As soon as we picked up speed, I let in the clutch and the engine sputtered in the cold night air but held.

Felix and Santa piled into the car and we roared off back to the fish market hoping nothing untoward had happened while we'd been away.

8

Once again I drove up to the warehouse, stopping just short of the doors.

We hurried up to the man way, Felix carrying little Martin and Jimbo holding my hand. We stopped at the sight of giant scratches in the wood. The Snarl had raked the doors in its attempt to gain access. Chunks of wood lay on the ground where it had spat them out as it ripped at the doors with its teeth.

Misgiving clutched at my heart. Apart from concern for the reindeer and the cats, Sam was my brother. Only one way to find out. I knocked on the door and called out. The door creaked open and Sam stood there. In one piece. Thank goodness. The cats broke their enclave and clowdered around us. Even the reindeer took a few paces away from their refuge behind the sleigh.

"Well?" they all chorused.

"Sorted," I said, while Santa gave the thumbs up.

With Santa and Felix interrupting me from time to time, I explained the plan to the reindeer, leaving out the bit about the medallions being only placebos. Sam and I tied them round the reindeers' necks while Santa anointed their wounds with the magic unguent. We had one item left to explain: Felix's role for the rest of the night.

"My friend Felix is a shape shifter," I told them as they gathered round me and stared at me with their round anxious eyes.

"So?" said Rudolf. "We've met them before?"

"Not like this. You mustn't be afraid. You realize we have to have something strong and fierce to combat the Snarl?"

They nodded their heads and their bells jingled.

"What is the fiercest animal you can think of?" I asked them.

"A lion... A polar bear... A tiger," came the answers.

"Two big cats and a bear. He's not one of those. What about a spotted big cat?"

"Oh no," said Dancer shrinking back behind the others. "He isn't a leopard, is he?"

Felix stepped forwards and bowed.

"I'm afraid so. But tonight I'm here to use the power of my claws and fangs in your defense against the Snarl. I'm going to thwart its every move and kill it if I can."

The reindeer looked at Santa for reassurance. He nodded. They turned to Donner, the leader of their team.

Donner winked at me. "I trust Mpenzi Munro," he said. "She wouldn't have gone to all this trouble just to let her friend eat us up."

"I see why you're their leader, Donner," I said and stroked him. "Is everyone agreed? We really don't have time to waste."

A full carillon of bells met my question.

"Good," I said. "While Santa and I harness you to the

sleigh, Felix will shift into his leopard form. The High Council of the White Witches have given him the magic power for tonight to fly alongside your sleigh as a defensive escort."

"What about me?" asked Sam.

"Your job is to pick up the presents and put them back in the sleigh. Jimbo will help. Then drive the car to the mayor's house and wait for us to join you for dinner there. If anything happens to delay us, you'll still be able to have Christmas dinner with Emmanuelle. Jimbo's coming with us."

"I am?" Jimbo asked as if he couldn't believe his good luck. "In Santa's sleigh?"

Santa pulled him into a hug. "Couldn't do without you, young man."

In no time Felix, the reindeer, the presents and Santa were ready. We said goodbye to Neptune and his tribe. Sam and I opened the main doors to make way for the sleigh and the reindeer. Felix padded out into the snow to guard the front of the warehouse.

Santa called out, "We'll have to fly the sleigh out. The runners won't slide on the rough concrete floor. I need you to warn me about the height clearance, Penzi."

I hastened across to join Felix. He scanned away from the building while I looked towards the doors. Santa climbed into his sleigh and clicked his tongue. Rudolf rose into the air first, followed by the four pairs of reindeer in harness. Last to leave the floor was the heavy sleigh. Santa held his magic rig at the hover for a few seconds while he lined the sleigh up with the doors, then with a great whoosh it swept out into the open air with Santa's head clearing the top of the doorway by an inch.

I climbed onto Felix's back and he shrugged his leopard's shoulders to boost me up onto Rudolf. We were ready for the next 180 degrees of Santa's journey around the world.

"Ho, ho, ho!" cried Santa.

Off we soared up into the night sky until Sam was a tiny little figure way below us in the snow.

9

———

For the rest of the night we flew up and down the degrees of longitude, landing on roofs of all shapes and sizes, visiting families, orphanages, hospitals and juvenile detention centers. Every time we returned to the Arctic Circle we filled up with presents in Lapland. Felix did his part fending off repeated assaults by the invisible Snarl as it swooped in from unexpected directions. Over Nova Scotia, we ran into a heavy sea fog and would have been in difficulty without Rudolf's red nose to show us the way.

Santa had to drive his team hard to make up for the time we'd lost. With all the magic in the world we couldn't slow the rotation of the Earth. By half past four in the morning we were flying northwards, returning from our last trip. The Snarl hadn't attacked for several degrees of latitude now. We'd covered the stretch of the Pacific where the International Date Line zigzags round far flung islands and were approaching the most westerly offshoots of Alaska, thinking ourselves home safe when the unthinkable happened.

Felix had been flying along our left flank. He suddenly tucked in his legs, swung around until he was pointing south and performed a perfect victory roll with his long tail streaming out behind him. He flew behind the sleigh and executed another victory roll along our right flank. And that did it.

10

F*elix*

To this day, I don't know what got into me. A mixture of self-congratulatory over confidence that our mission had ended successfully with all the presents delivered and relief that the Snarl had given up?

But, of course, it hadn't. I still can't work out whether it found my victory rolls provocative — a challenge it couldn't refuse — or whether it was my widdershins flight around the sleigh that called down the evil again. Looking back, I should have realized how dangerous any anti-clockwise movement would be. Gwinny had warned us that all magic had to be performed clockwise, but I hadn't wanted to fly across the front of the reindeer in case I startled them and made Rudolf throw Penzi. I paid dearly for my mistake.

The Snarl came out of nowhere, drenching me in its foul vapors. I tried to avoid it, but it dived on me with a great flapping of invisible wings and an earsplitting screech.

It assailed me with its full arsenal: claws, tentacles, fangs, barbed tails, beaks; all of which I only sensed. I fought desperately knowing that if it won this battle, there would never be another Christmas for the children of the world, but I'd been caught unawares and was exhausted.

Some part of its fearful anatomy seized me by my scruff. I struggled to withstand the involuntary reflex built into all cats to curl up and submit to being carried, but my muscles wouldn't respond and I hung slackly in its grasp. The monster soared higher and higher, spiraling upwards towards the clouds. The coastline appeared below me and as the Snarl flew ever higher, Mount Hesperus came into view. The air at nine thousand feet was breathable by me in my snow leopard form, but the situation was dire. I began to struggle against my cub like behavior. I wriggled and shrugged in an effort to dislodge the Snarl's hold on me. To no avail. On the Snarl climbed. In the distance over to my right, the peak of Mount Denali, the highest mountain in the Alaska Range rose above us, its snowy slopes tinged pink as the Earth turned towards the sun. My breath was coming harsh and disjointed, my lungs straining for oxygen. Seventeen thousand feet is the natural habitat of snow leopards. Anything over that would kill me and leave the Snarl free to attack Santa's sleigh. I had to do something. As a last resort I did what many prey animals do, I feigned death. I ceased fighting back and let myself go limp. I slowed my breathing down as much as I dared without passing out.

The Snarl let out a jubilant screech and dropped me. Down I plummeted, falling fast through many thousands of feet until I got my wits about me again. I splayed out my legs and my tail and summoned up my faith in the magic of the High Council of the Guild of White Witches. They had told me I could fly for this one night, so fly I did. My descent slowed as the magic began to work against the power of gravity. Below me growing larger by the second, Santa's sleigh was flying round in slow circles, marking the spot where I'd disappeared. I spiraled down until I was alongside Penzi and Rudolf once more.

The reindeers gave me little grunts of welcome. Penzi let go of Rudolf's reins to clap her hands. Santa called out, "Homeward bound. Ho, ho, ho!" and clicked his team onwards.

The Snarl's plan to kill me by depriving me of oxygen had failed and it had flown off. A problem for another day, I said to myself as I gulped down the life-giving oxygen all around me. Santa turned his team to the east to set Penzi and me back down in Beaucoup-sur-Mer for our Christmas dinner with the mayor. All's well that ends well, but I had reckoned without the evil power behind the Snarl.

The Snarl dive-bombed me as we were flying over the Atlantic. Although its attack was unexpected, I was familiar with its tactics by now. As I fought it, I twisted and squirmed this way and that doing anything to stop it taking hold of my scruff again. This time I launched the offensive. Waiting until I sensed it swooping about below me, I jumped down through the air landing on it with all the force of my four mighty paws. My long claws latched onto something, I know not what part of the beast, and I held on with all my strength.

Then I took a risk. I shut down my magic ability to fly. Down we fell, spiraling out of control as gravity took us down to the ocean. The Snarl strove to fight the force of the earth's pull and gain height but my weight was too much for it. We plunged into the icy cold waves of the Northern Atlantic. Down we sank our combined weight and the force of our fall taking us through several fathoms. I'd taken a deep breath as we hit the water and I held it for my life's sake. As our dive tailed off, I slowly let my breath out to achieve neutral buoyancy and hung there deep in the sea until I felt the Snarl collapse in on itself. When I was sure there was no life left in it, I kicked sharply with my hind legs and rose up through the water. We, leopards, are strong swimmers. I paddled about until my lungs had recovered, then I summoned up the magic power to fly again and spiraled upwards matching the route of my descent.

"The Snarl is dead," I shouted out as Santa's sleigh came into view.

All the way back to France, the reindeer sang, "The Snarl is dead. Long live Felix."

Santa insisted I join him and Jimbo. Penzi hadn't come prepared with her broomstick, and so she couldn't fly to the sleigh. She unharnessed Rudolf who carried her over to us and she climbed in. Rudolf flew alongside us all the way back to the mayor's house.

11

Two things come to mind about that last leg of the journey. I asked Felix how he'd known what to do to kill the Snarl.

"I didn't know. I guessed and took a risk. It was all to do with oxygen. The Snarl tried to fly me so high I'd die from oxygen starvation. It could breathe at those heights. That was its biological specialty. I thought it unlikely it had a second one. So I dragged it down under the sea."

"So you were lucky that it worked?"

Felix answered with a chuckle. "*Absolument*, as the mayor would say. When you're in a situation like that, anything you try is better than accepting death."

The second thing was to do with a remark Santa had made before we started off on our delivery round. It had niggled me all night. He'd said he and his reindeer didn't visit all children on Christmas Eve. When I'd asked him what he meant, he said he'd tell me later. So I asked him what he'd meant.

"I don't mean the children who celebrate Christmas on other dates, such as Boxing Day or Twelfth Night for example. And I don't mean children whose families don't celebrate Christmas but celebrate other religious or seasonal holidays. I mean children who never receive gifts at all because they're living in poverty or caught up in situations beyond their control. You must have noticed we didn't visit all children tonight?"

"Yes, I did, but I suppose I'm conditioned to accept that some children miss out at Christmas."

Santa frowned down at me. "Is that right?"

"Of course not. Anyway, why don't you take presents to every child? You're the one with the toy factories." I said rather more sharply than I should have done.

"It's simple economics. Parents with enough money buy shares in my toy factories. Their children receive presents as a dividend. If a child has no parents or his or her parents are too poor, I can't deliver a present to them. There are many aid and charitable agencies who help to fill in the gap, but it's nowhere near enough."

We'd over flown many areas without stopping to make a delivery: refugee camps, war zones, inner cities and impoverished villages. What Santa said was true. Thousands of children would go without a present on Christmas morning.

"It's an impossible situation, Santa. What can an ordinary person do about it?"

Santa smiled and looked at Felix.

"Felix?"

"We could teach our children to give as well as receive."

"Good answer. What else can we do, Penzi?"

"The answer's obvious: raise the standard of living in the world, but I don't see how an ordinary person can do that."

"As long as the ordinary person accepts that it needs to

be done, one day I shall be delivering presents to every child. It's that hope that gets me up in the morning. Now, you are not to get depressed about this. You have both worked hard tonight to make sure that many of the world's children have presents tomorrow. That's a great achievement."

We didn't speak for the rest of the journey and soon the coast of France lay before us. Santa homed in on the sleepy little town of Beaucoup-sur-Mer and guided his team gently down to the road in front of the mayor's house. Felix and I said goodbye to the reindeer while Santa gave Jimbo a big hug.

We stood back as Santa called out, "Ho, ho, ho!" He clicked his tongue and the reindeers rose into the air and headed north for Lapland. We watched them till they were out of sight.

Felix sighed. "What a magical night. No one would believe it."

I looked at the time. "One o'clock. Time to release the *forget* spell."

I snapped my fingers and our time was once more in synch with the rest of the town of Beaucoup-sur-Mer.

Felix, Jimbo and I hurried up the drive to find Sam just arriving in our car.

"Merry Christmas," he said, jumping out to join in a group hug. "Did all the children receive their presents?"

I nodded. "It was fun rescuing Santa, wasn't it?"

"*Fun* isn't the word I'd use, boss," said Felix. "It was touch and go for a moment there, you know."

"Felix was awfully brave," Jimbo said. "You should have seen him fighting the Snarl. That monster was the scariest thing in the world. I hope it's really dead."

"Oh, don't be so dreary, you two. It's Christmas."

The four of us linked arms and walked up to the front door to join the Bonhomie family for a French Christmas dinner.

THE END OF BOOK FIVE
French Country Murders

~

Now, you may wish to read the first chapter of the next book in this series,
The Witch who Foiled the Plot.

~

THE WITCH WHO FOILED THE PLOT
CHAPTER ONE

Five months without a murder... and counting. Here we were in mid-March with the spring bursting out in our new garden. No sign of evil anywhere. Birds singing, trees burgeoning into leaf and bees busy with the first flowers. Over the winter Beaucoup-sur-Mer had recovered from the spate of killings that had rocked our little French seaside town in the late summer and early autumn after our arrival in our new home at *Les Dragons*.

Our father's will had laid down that we had to move from our then home in Notting Hill Gate in London, England, to his second home in France. It had been an unwelcome upheaval for all three of us: for my brother Jimbo, who was only nine and had to start school in France without being able to speak French, for my brother Sam, who at eighteen had wanted to go off and do his thing but now had to stay with the family and help us adapt our lives to living in France, and for me, a new barrister with my first portfolio of clients. The only members of the family who didn't seem to mind the move were our two German shepherds, Zig and Zag.

Arriving in France, we had come upon our long lost mother Gwinny who had deserted us all seven years previously. Jimbo had been ecstatic; Sam and I less so, forgiveness being good for the soul but hard to come by.

Along the way, the three of us had gained a friend in Felix who'd been sent from the Middle Congo by my father, Sir Archibald Munro, to be my bodyguard. I needed one. The wicked witch doctor of the Wazini back in Africa was out to kill me in revenge against my father's support of the government there, in their campaign to stamp out the murderous Leopardmen.

Thereby hangs a tale as they say. When delivered at our door in Beaucoup-sur-Mer, Felix was a handsome Savannah cat, but he was a shifter who could morph from cat to leopard to man in any order. He had taken me by surprise the first time I came upon his human form. But as he said, as a supernatural myself it was time I got used to such strange happenings.

After seven months I was coming to terms with finding out I was a white witch. At first I'd been rebellious, thinking all that magic stuff was nonsense. As a barrister with a mind trained to analyze facts and nuances of the law, it took me some time to come to an understanding that I had been *called*; that using magic in the fight of good against evil was my vocation in life. At first, it had been difficult for me. At twenty-five, I was a late starter and had a lot of catching up to do. Being dyslexic had only added to the difficulty of learning the spells I needed. My father had sent me my mother's *Book of Spells* along with his will. Faced with such a vast amount of material to learn, I'd been advised by Felix to tackle the spells as and when they were needed. So far, the High Council of the Guild of White Witches, who monitored my progress, had been happy with that approach. I hadn't needed to learn a new spell since our adventure at Christmastime when we'd given Santa a helping hand. However, with a performance review due any day from the High Council, I might have to up the pace of my studying.

All this was running through my mind as I sat in the kitchen with Felix having a mid-morning cup of tea and one of my favorite chocolate éclairs.

"Penny for your thoughts," said Felix.

"Shouldn't it be a Euro or a centime?" I replied.

"Some things don't translate. Go on. Tell me what's giving you that far-away look."

"I was thinking about how far we've come since our family moved over here to France. The money spent on the garden is beginning to pay off. Look out of the window as it comes alive with the onset of spring. Jimbo's doing well at school and will soon speak a more colloquial French than either of us. Life is peaceful at last. That monsoon of evil that swept over Beaucoup-sur-Mer after our arrival here has blown itself out."

"Sam's not too happy and you, yourself, still have to find a means of earning a living."

"Sam's time will come. This year is giving him a chance to decide what he wants to do with his life. Although the gap year was forced on him by my father's will, it has been good for Sam."

"And you, boss? What are you going to do with yourself for the rest of your life?"

"I've been giving it a lot of thought recently. Should I stick with a life in the law, undertake the necessary study to qualify as an advocate in France? The whole philosophy of the law here is so different from the Anglo-Saxon model.

I'm not sure I could get my head or my heart around it. Then there's the antiques business."

"How about private investigator?" asked Felix with a wink.

I rolled my eyes before I could stop myself. "That was forced on me, I didn't choose it. I don't want to spend my life peering into the worst aspects of people's actions."

"You can't deny you sought and found justice for the victims."

I sighed. Felix was right, but it was dirty work even so.

Felix put his hand over mine. "Don't sweat it, Penzi. It will come to you. There's no harm in taking a few months off after all the hard years of study you've put in while bringing up your two brothers."

I turned my head to look at Gwinny who was standing at the sink peeling potatoes for lunch. I was sure I'd heard her sniffle.

"Gwinny," I called out, "Felix wasn't getting at you."

She looked over her shoulder at us and wiped her eyes with her spare hand. "Don't you worry about me. It's these onions."

Felix and I exchanged a glance. My mother had been waiting for us in Beaucoup-sur-Mer when we'd arrived the previous summer. She'd been the one to renovate the house for us and since then she'd been living with us, much to Jimbo's joy. Felix had rebuked me several times in the past for being so unforgiving towards her for the seven years she'd left me to care for my siblings.

She dropped the paring knife in the sink with a splash, pulled out the chair at the end of the table and sat down drying her hands on her apron. She put out a hand to cover mine and Felix's.

"Penzi, take your time," she said. "The universe will

give you the answer when you're ready. I wish I could take back the last seven years and start over, but I can't."

To my dismay I'd flinched before I could stop myself when she placed her hand on mine. I quickly covered our three hands with my other one and gave hers a squeeze, hoping she hadn't noticed my reaction. My heart was still closed to her, but I didn't want to cause her pain. My coldness was my problem, not hers. I had to work on forgiveness.

"Thanks Gwinny," I said. "I hope you know how much we value your help now that you're living with us."

She gave me a faint smile, withdrew her hand and returned to the sink.

"Oh," she said as she looked out of the window. "Martine's here. Right on time for her morning coffee."

Martine Courier was our postwoman and something of a family friend. She'd proved invaluable on many occasions with her knowledge of local gossip and personalities. In France, postmen have a duty to report if they consider anyone needs assistance. That makes them inquisitive by nature and a useful resource for a private investigator.

She rapped on the front door and bustled into the kitchen taking the seat vacated by Gwinny only a few moments before. It took her a few seconds to throw our mail down on the table and settle her large bulk into the chair.

Gwinny placed a cup of hot coffee before her and signaled to Felix to pass her the box of éclairs.

Martine wriggled to get comfortable, pulled down her tunic and reached for one saying, "I really shouldn't but I can't resist."

She took a bite. "Good. Not as good as Tidot's were, but not bad."

On top of the usual Monday morning pile of publicity

catalogs lay an A4 manila envelope, an official looking missive. I raised my eyebrows at Felix and he nodded back. Recent history had made me wary of such letters. I waited with impatience for Martine to push the mail towards me, but she carried on munching her éclair quite oblivious of my anxiety. The pastry demolished, she downed her cup of coffee in a couple of mouthfuls. At last she raised her eyes and caught mine.

She gave an embarrassed titter and pushed the pile towards me. "I'm sorry, Penzi. I'm such a gourmande. Forgive me."

I was no closer to knowing what the envelope said. I could make out my name but that was all. I extracted the sheaf of publicity papers from the bottom and passed them to Gwinny. The letters, half a dozen or so, I handed to Felix to read noticing as I did so that there were two large manila envelopes, not one.

Felix picked up the two envelopes. "The first one's for you, Penzi, but the other one's addressed to me. Who could know I'm living here with you? The postmarks are French."

"Well, open them then," I said as I reached behind me for a knife with which to slit them open and passed it to him.

I waited with my stomach muscles tightening. Official letters never brought good news. Were the authorities checking up on Felix? He had no legal standing as far as I knew. He had immigrated into France as a cat, not a human being, and we had faked his application for a UK passport.

Felix pulled out the letter and scanned it quickly, the furrow between his eyes deepening as he read down the page. He flipped over to the second without looking up at me. It had to be bad. I dug my nails into my tightly wrapped palms.

He flicked the first page back over the second and stared down at the letter while he gathered his thoughts.

"What is it, Felix? You're scaring me," I asked him unable to keep the note of apprehension out of my voice.

At last, he glanced across at me. "It's from the Ministry."

"What do they want?"

"It's about our last case."

"Are we in trouble? Did we break a law?"

Felix relaxed enough to chuckle. "You know we did, but that's not it. Let me check the one addressed to me before I tell you anything."

Martine held her cup out to Gwinny for a refill. In my anxiety I'd forgotten she was still sitting there enjoying her usual break from her postal delivery routine. I wanted to warn Felix not to say anything in front of her. *Pas devant les enfants* came to mind, but that wouldn't work because Martine was French, so I gave Felix a hefty kick under the table.

"Ouch!" he said rubbing his shin and glaring at me. "There's no need for that. I'm taking my time because I want to be sure I understand all this legal French properly."

Martine was reaching back to take her refill from Gwinny, so I risked a jerk of my head in her direction and put my finger to my mouth to say *watch it*.

Felix took the hint, rising to his feet and saying, "We need a dictionary for this. Let's go into the study, Penzi."

I pushed back my chair and made it to the kitchen door before Felix, tossing off a quick *au'voir* to Martine over my shoulder on the way out.

As soon as the study door was closed, I turned round to Felix and punched him on the arm. "Stop being such a rotter and tell me what the letters say. I'm getting more and more anxious."

"Chill, boss. I want to be sure about this before I tell you what they say."

I hurried across to my father's chair and sat down. Felix pulled a French-English dictionary down from the bookshelf and spent a few minutes rifling through the pages, giving a slight grunt every time he found the word he wanted and scribbling it down above the typed French.

Satisfied at last that he understood the content of the letters, he put down his pen, shut the dictionary with a thump and shot me a beaming smile.

"You'll never guess," he said.

"Of course, I won't. Tell me what they say. I can't stand the suspense. Good news or bad?"

"I wouldn't be smiling if it was bad news, would I?" he said reaching across the desk for my hands and holding them tightly.

He stared deep into my eyes and said, "Mpenzi Munro, you are now officially a millionaire."

"What?" I gasped. "What on earth are you talking about?"

"The letters are from the Ministry informing us of our share of the reward for solving the case of the oyster farmers. The four of us, Izzy, Garth, you and I, are granted over two million Euros each."

I blinked and blinked again while the import of Felix's news sank in. No more money problems.

"For real?" I whispered as the breath whooshed out of me.

Felix nodded. "Both of us. We're set up for life."

"I can't believe it. I can make sure Sam and Jimbo get the education and training they want. I'll be able to take care of Gwinny as she grows older... and help other people. It's magic."

I snatched my hands away and leapt to my feet. Throwing my arms in the air I did a victory dance whooping, "Yes, yes. Maaaaaagic."

The door to the study opened and Gwinny stepped in with Martine peering over her shoulder.

"What's going on in here? Are you all right?" she asked.

"Never better," I answered not breaking off from my jig of happiness.

"Well?" she asked.

Felix put his finger to his lips. I didn't need his warning. There was no way I wanted Martine to know about our exotic windfall. It would be all round the town and we'd be besieged by demands for financial help. And Gwinny shouldn't know either. But what to say? I had to think of something.

I stopped prancing about.

"Izzy has managed to persuade her friend who works in the Louvre to come and appraise all those paintings in the *brocante*. He's coming next month."

"Your reaction seems a bit over the top, but I suppose it's progress. It's time you started earning some money," Gwinny said as she left the room pushing Martine backwards into the hall.

"Phew!" said Felix stifling a laugh. "We nearly gave the game away there."

I took my seat again. "We can't let anyone know. We'll never have a moment's peace."

"I agree with you there. But we have a more serious problem than keeping all this secret."

"What's that?" I asked him.

"What are we going to do with the rest of our lives if we don't need to earn a living?"

As usual, Felix had put his finger right on the crux of the matter. What indeed?

~

I hope you enjoyed this first chapter of
The Witch who Foiled the Plot
You will find this book available for sale at your favorite bookseller. Links on my website - KatiePenryn.com

~

NOTE FROM KATIE PENRYN

THE PIXIE DUST EFFECT

If you enjoyed this book, I'd love it if you'd pass your enjoyment on to others by leaving a review. Reviews are like pixie dust. Pure magic! They help other readers decide whether to read my books, and they pump me full of endorphins, firing up my imagination and making me thump away at the old keyboard with renewed enthusiasm to get my stories out faster.

Join my Readers' Group on my website and receive a free coloring book suitable for all ages, KatiePenryn.com, or on my Facebook page, Facebook.com/KatiePenryn.Author

Available at your favorite bookseller. Links on my website - KatiePenryn.com

French Country Murders

Book 1: The Witch who Couldn't Spell
Book 2: The Witch who Loved Eclairs

Book 3: The Witch who Got the Blues
Book 4: The Witch who Found a Pearl
Book 5: The Witch who Saved Christmas
Book 6: The Witch who Foiled the Plot
Book 7: The Witch who Hated Halloween
Book 8: The Witch who Risked the Shot
Book 9: The Witch who Picked a Poppy
Book 10: The Witch who Forged a Monet
- *Nov 2021*
Book 11: The Witch who Tipped the Scales
- *Mar 2022*

This series is also available in Large Print and Ebook.

Our Man in Mazita

Book 1: Beau—ootiful Soo—oop!
Book 2 : Something Spotted
Book 3: Something Rotten
Book 4: Christmas in Mazita

To view these and my other books, please visit my website, KatiePenryn.com, or my Author Page on your favorite bookseller's site.

You can write to me at katiepenryn@gmail.com. I love hearing from you. Knowing that there's someone out there who has brought my book to life through their own imagination is a wonderful feeling. I answer all emails and Facebook messages personally.

12.viii.21

GLOSSARY

French words and expressions:

absolument – absolutely
mes amis – my friends
amour propre – lit. self-love, used in English, self-respect
la bavette – a thin cheaper steak, skirt
bonne idée – that's a good idea
bonsoir – good evening
BB – Brigitte Bardot, a beloved and sexy French filmstar of the '50s and '60s
une brocante – something between an antiques shop and a bric-à-brac shop
une casse-croûte – a snack, literally "break-crust", meaning a piece broken off a loaf of bread
ça suffit! – that's enough!
le cafard – lit. cockroach, the French for the blues (misery not music!)
le cantonnier – the gardener, general handyman of a village – from the word "canton" – several communes make up one canton.

Combien? – how much?

une commune – is a level of administrative division in the French Republic. French communes are analogous to civil townships and incorporated municipalities in the United States. The United Kingdom has no exact equivalent, as communes resemble districts in urban areas, but are closer to parishes in rural areas where districts are much larger. Communes are based on historical geographic communities or villages and have received significant powers of governance to manage the populations and land of the geographic area covered. The communes are the fourth-level administrative divisions of France. Each commune has a mayor.

"Dames" – ladies' cloakroom/bathroom

déjà-vu – used in English, means "already seen"

un demi – lit. a half, used for drinks especially beer/lager meaning half a liter

deux-chevaux – lit. two-horses, a little French car Citroën with two h.p.

les dragons – the dragons

faisant les cents pas – lit. doing a hundred steps, pacing up and down

en famille – used in English; to do something as a family, together

et alors? – what next ? So ?

épuisé(e) - exhausted

la farine – flour

un gendarme – see item below, a policeman who has a military background

la gendarmerie – the station were the gendarmes hang out, roughly speaking like a police station, but the gendarmes are not policemen as such. The Gendarmerie Nationale is part of the French armed forces. It has the primary responsibility for policing smaller towns and rural areas, as well as the armed forces and military installations, airport security and shipping ports. Being a military force, the gendarmerie has a highly centralized organization structure. It is under the control of both the Ministry of Defense and the Ministry of the Interior (as far as its civil duties are concerned).

faux-filet – lit. a false fillet steak, a sirloin steak

un gâteau – a cake

kir royale – a French cocktail, a variation on Kir. It consists of crème de cassis topped with champagne

le livret de famille – family record kept by the mayor's office

une madeleine– a buttery little sponge cake usually shaped like a scallop shell

le maire – the mayor, the administrator of a commune. He is voted for by the rate-paying residents, including non-citizens.

la mairie – the mayor's office; in a large town or city, this would be the Town Hall.

mais oui – but yes, of course

Maître – lit. master, used to France as an honorary title for a lawyer/advocate

malheuresement – unfortunately

Le Marché de Sables – Market of the Sands

la maternelle – nursery school

le méchoui – a spit roasted pig or sheep (from the Arabic)

le métier – profession, occupation

merci mille fois – thank-you a thousand times

le merguez – long thin highly spiced sausage

naturellement! – naturally!

des objets-d'art – used in English; small pieces of art such as sculptures, enameled jewellery boxes

Le Palais des Blues – the Blues Palace

une pâtisserie – a cake shop and/or a pastry

ma/mon pauvre petit(e) – my poor little one
pineau – is an aperitif from the Charente/Dordogne departments. It is a fortified wine of the same strength as sherry and comes in a red or a white version. Often served over ice.
Punaise! – lit. a shield-shaped green bug that stinks when touched. Used as a mild swear word
Salut! – Hi ! Informal
Sympa – an adjective meaning companionable, friendly, an okay person
thé à l'anglais – tea English style with milk
La Toussaint – All Saints' Day
tout de suite – at once, immediately
trop dégueulasse! – too disgusting!
Vade mecum – the Latin for "come with me"; often used for an indispensable item such as a diary, travel guide

Other references:

Banksy- is an anonymous England-based street artist. His satirical street art and subversive epigrams combine dark humor with graffiti executed in a distinctive stenciling technique.
dolmen – is a prehistoric arrangement of large stone blocks, with one horizontally straddling two uprights to make an arch. Their origin and use are uncertain, but they were probably the entrance to tombs which have since disappeared.
Laphroaig – the golden single malt scotch whisky from the Isle of Islay in the Hebrides, famous for its distinctive peaty flavor
Leopardmen – these men are part of African folklore
Send someone to Coventry –an English expression meaning

to stop speaking to someone, i.e. stop social contact
with them

Sowhat – is an anonymous Parisian street artist

Venn diagram – A diagram using overlapping circles to
show areas of correspondence